Baby Din is Hiding

by Jay Dale

illustrated by Jacqueline East

"Baby Dinosaur!"
shouted Father Dinosaur.
"Where are you?"

2

"I am hiding,"
said Baby Dinosaur.

"I am coming to look
for you,"
said Father Dinosaur.
"I will look inside this log."

Father Dinosaur
looked inside the log.

"I can not see you,"
said Father Dinosaur.
"Where are you?"

"I am hiding,"
said Baby Dinosaur.
"You can not see me."

"I am coming to look
for you,"
said Father Dinosaur.
"I will look
in the little trees."

Father Dinosaur
looked in the little trees.
He looked and looked.

"I can see you!"
shouted Father Dinosaur.

Baby Dinosaur ran away.
She went inside a big cave.

"Baby Dinosaur!"
shouted Father Dinosaur.
"Where are you?"

15

"I am hiding,"
said Baby Dinosaur.
"You can not see me."